Love!

KOKOPELLI

the

& Butterfly

by Michael Sterns

Color & Special Effects by Gayle Deal
Line Drawings by Joseph V. Cioffi

Copyright ©2000 by Michael Sterns

Library of Congress Catalog Card Number: 00-108566
ISBN 0-9672533-1-4

Printed in Canada

Kichita Productions
2227 Shadehill Court
Tampa, FL 33612
kichitabeats.freetailer.com

Book orders: www.kokopelli-butterfly.com
813-931-5148

Sterns, Michael.
       Kokopelli & the Butterfly / by Michael Sterns ; line
drawings by Joseph v Cioffi & special effects by Gayle
Deal. -- 3rd ed.
       p. cm.
       Audience: Ages 4 & up
       LCCN 00-108566
       SUMMARY: When Kokopelli was shown a butterfly in an
ornate cage, he was struck by the butterfly's beauty,
but saddened by the caged animal's suffering. The
people in the village were more concerned with showing
their treasure than they were with the butterfly's
plight, so Kokopelli liberated the butterfly, causing an
amazing transformation.
       ISBN 0-9672533-1-4
       1. Kokopelli (Pueblo deity)--Juvenile fiction.
2. Nature--Juvenile fiction. 3. Conflict management--
Juvenile fiction. 4. Interpersonal relations--Juvenile
fiction. I. Cioffi, Joseph V. II. Deal, Gayle.
III. Title.

PZ7.S83895Ko 2000   [E]
                QBI00-901509

Dedicated to the loving child in all of us

FROM THE AUTHOR...

Thank you so much for picking up this copy of Kokopelli & the Butterfly. In your hands you are holding the fruit of over five years of incredible collaboration by many wonderful people. I would like to thank my family, friends, and community for their eternal support and encouragement. I couldn't have done it without them! I would like to personally thank my fantastically talented artistic cohorts, Gayle Deal and Joseph Cioffi, for believing in me. My wish is that this book serves as an inspiration to all. Never give up on your dreams. As cliché as it may sound, this book is proof that anything is possible if you keep moving toward what makes you passionate!

I am grateful for the opportunity to share my dream of compassion, hope and love for all of mankind. I'm inviting the world to join me on an endeavor of world peace, beginning with the most important person of all, our self. Treat yourself kindly, like we all treat children when we see them. Treat everyone with love and respect, forgive yourself if you falter, but do try again and again. Flood children with love, kindness, and knowledge.

We are here to love.

This is a book for adults and children alike. My wish is that it will find it's way onto as many coffee tables as in toy chests. My dream is that this book will act as a vehicle to help foster more high-quality interaction between adults and children. In turn, I hope that many parents will teach their children the love of reading by sharing Kokopelli & the Butterfly with them. The family reading experience is so valuable, where children grow skills in learning, creativity, imagination, and conversation in a perfectly nurturing environment. It is also a place where parents can "let go" of their daily concerns and get fully involved, carefree like a child, in a good story.

I purposely created this book the size it is so that you can have your arm around your child(ren) when you read together. I also alternated the sides the illustrations appear on, so if there is more than one child involved, they may share equally in the reading experience. I hope you'll agree that it's ideal for children of all ages, and with its illustrations, challenging vocabulary and poignant lessons, I encourage parents to use it as a teaching tool as well. Don't forget to add character voices, making it a fun and riveting experience for both parent and child.

My hope is that this book's message of environmentalism, appreciation of nature's beauty, tolerance of diversity and peaceful conflict resolution will be heard clearly by all. It's time for the global community to come together as one and take care of our selves, each other, and the Earth. We as adults want the same things we did as children. We all want to love and be loved. Let's learn from our children as we teach them. As we encourage our children to find their own way, let's not forget to remain loving, curious, and "in the moment" like them. We are all connected and have so much to gain in sharing with each other.

Please support educational, environmental, humanitarian, and artistic causes. Appreciate every precious moment of life, and most importantly, smile! Thank you all so much.

Love,

Michael Sterns
www.kokopelli-butterfly.com

Once upon a time, there was a mystical fellow named Kokopelli. His legend is well known among many native tribes around the world. Hundreds of years ago, from what is now North and South America all the way to the Pacific Islands, stories of Kokopelli's travels were told around many campfires. Long ago in lands now known as Europe, Indonesia, Africa and Australia, boys and girls of all ages gathered around the elder tribesmen to hear of Kokopelli's adventures.

Kokopelli was quite an interesting fellow. He was a wanderer by choice, delighting in the overwhelming beauty of nature that constantly surrounded him. Hundreds of years ago, most of the land was in its original state, untouched and many times unseen by even a single human. Kokopelli loved to stroll through the green, misty forests and sunny, flower-speckled meadows. Standing on towering coastal cliffs, he loved to listen to the thundering surf as it crashed on the rocks below. He smiled as he breathed the fresh, clean air and listened to the various calls of the animals. He stood in awe of the majestic mountains above him, and then drank from their cold, clear streams.

ecause he was a gentle soul, Kokopelli lived
in harmony with all the humans and animals
he met. He never harmed the animals, for he
felt all living beings deserved love and respect.
He showed them how to plant trees to replace the
ones they cut down for their buildings and
fires, because he knew that trees provide
air for the Earth and habitat for her creatures.

He taught every tribe he could to grow all the food they needed, and to take care of Mother Earth in return. He encouraged them to fertilize the land with any uneaten food, creating rich soil to grow strong future crops. Kokopelli also taught people to remake things they would normally throw away into helpful objects, making him the first man on Earth to recycle.

H e begged them to care for nearby lakes and streams, keeping them free of pollution because he knew that water is one of Earth's most precious resources. He taught people to use only the water they needed and not to waste a single precious drop, because all living things share water and need it to survive.

But most important, Kokopelli taught them to love one another, showing them how to settle disputes by talking them out peacefully, rather than arguing or fighting. He taught the men of the tribes he encountered to remake their weapons into tools, so that they would never be used to harm another human again. Kokopelli generated more kindness than any person the tribespeople had ever met.

Kokopelli enjoyed his life of travel and adventure, and acquired many skills over time. He was an incredible magician, and could conjure spells and mystify his audiences with amazing tricks.

A wonderful musician as well, he played the pipes and drums with all his might and created more delightful music than ten men could. He danced wildly, sometimes to convey a story, other times just to entertain his tribal friends.

He danced to please the spirits in order to bring rain to make the crops grow or to help the sick become well again. Whatever the reason, it was always the most magnificent dance the tribes had ever seen. When Kokopelli sang, man and beast came from miles around to hear the fantastic music that echoed throughout the forests and canyons.

Kokopelli reflected his inner happiness through his friendly eyes and radiant smile. Throughout his life, Kokopelli had met many wonderful women, but he had never fallen in love. He knew instinctively that when he finally met the woman of his dreams, both of them would recognize their destiny together in one magical moment. He looked forward to that day with excitement, as his special princess would be one whom he could share his deepest hopes, dreams and wondrous adventures with. She would laugh and cry with him in all the glory of life's amazing experiences. She would be a magnificent lady and he could hardly wait until the day they would meet.

One beautiful spring day, Kokopelli walked through the foothills of a vast mountain range he had been exploring the previous week.

He saw wisps of smoke from tribal campfires trailing skyward in the valley below. The surrounding forest was lush, green and beautiful, full of gigantic trees and ferns. The forest was alive with the calls of the animals, and as he strolled along, he soon found himself on a footpath that led to the tribe's camp.

Kokopelli, like always, befriended the tribe because of his kind, caring ways. That night Kokopelli helped the men and women of the camp with the preparation of a scrumptious meal. He shared exotic foods from faraway lands, and when the feast had ended he put on a display of dancing, music, singing, storytelling and magic. He watched as the couples of the tribe danced with each other, smiling and holding their babies. They all talked and laughed as the stars brightened in the moonless sky. It pleased Kokopelli to see his new friends so happy, snuggling by the campfire.

It had been a great day, and after everyone had turned in for a well-deserved sleep, he lay by the fire staring up at the unbelievably clear sky. As he looked up at the millions of bright, twinkling stars he thought about the lady of his dreams, wondering where she might be. Smiling, he imagined what she might be doing, what she looked like when she laughed, and how the soothing sound of her voice would softly drift him into a blissful slumber. As these heartwarming thoughts floated through his mind, Kokopelli fell asleep.

Kokopelli was awakened in the cool morning air by the laughter of the tribe's children as they splashed in the clear blue lake. Delicious breakfast smells from the camp's fires filled his nostrils as he stretched and yawned, a smile brightening his face as he watched the children play. The tribe was already very busy as they had begun their daily chores and activities.

He greeted his new friends with a hearty "Good morning!" as he strolled along the lakeside.

One of the young men of the tribe, with a bright grin, approached him and said, "Hello, Kokopelli. The chief requests your presence immediately. He has something wonderful he would like to show you!"

Sensing the excitement in the young man's voice, Kokopelli rushed over with him to the chief's hut.

As Kokopelli approached, he saw that a large crowd had gathered inside and was obviously awaiting his arrival. He wondered what was causing this much excitement. As he drew nearer, the crowd parted, opening a path that led to the chief. The tribe's leader was proudly seated on a large, bear-shaped throne, his face beaming.

"Welcome, Kokopelli!" the chief boomed.

In a humble voice, with a slight bow, Kokopelli replied, "Thank you, chief, for welcoming me into your beautiful village. Your hospitality is greatly appreciated. It has been such a nice experience getting to know your tribe. I was told you have something to show me?"

The chief smiled and nodded, glancing at an object illuminated by a beam of light that shined through a hole in the ceiling. The chief explained that in return for Kokopelli's kindness, the tribe wanted him to see their most prized possession.

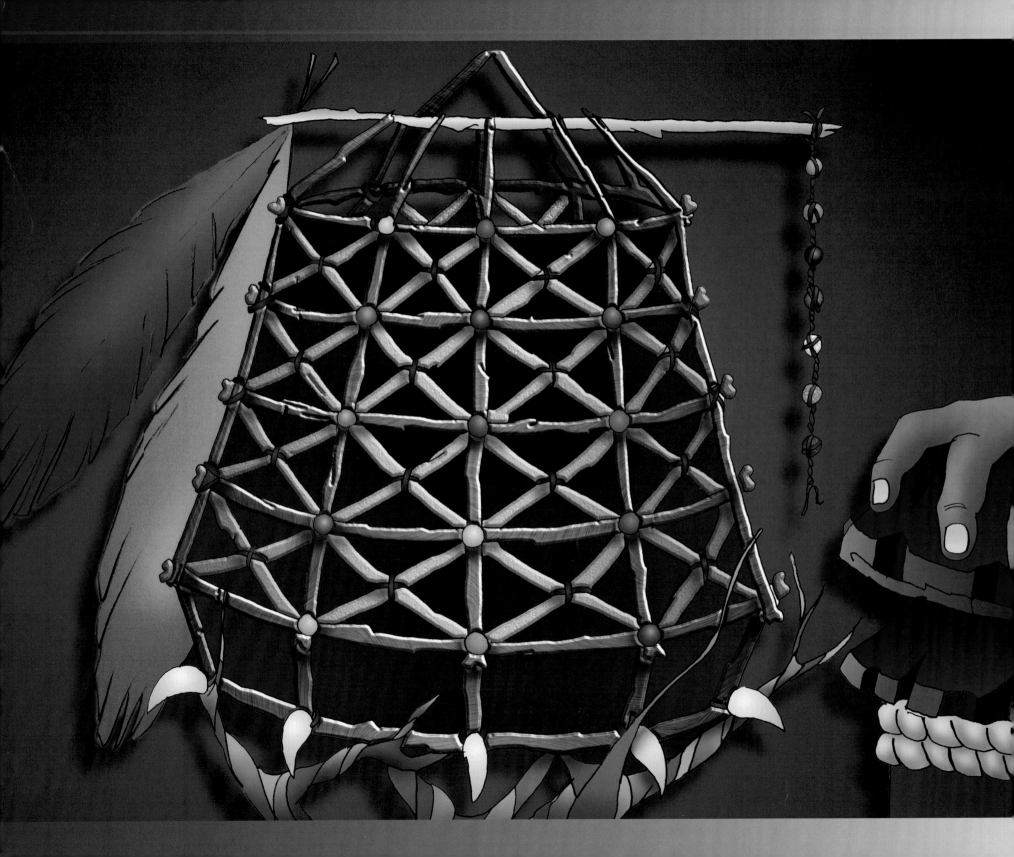

The object was concealed with an elaborately decorated deerskin cover. The crowd grew quiet as the chief slowly removed the shroud. He then displayed one of the most unusual objects that Kokopelli had ever seen. It was a small, ornate cage. The bars of the cage were constructed of animal bones and teeth, fastened together with small strips of leather. The bars had been patiently carved and dyed with bright colors. The cage was adorned with the feathers of the forest's birds. What Kokopelli saw next caused his mouth to drop open with surprise and sadness.

Inside was the most breathtakingly beautiful creature he had ever seen. He was awestruck that something this splendid even existed on Earth. It also saddened him because he could see that the animal inside was suffering, yet these people only cared about impressing Kokopelli. Inside the cage was a gorgeous butterfly, with the largest, most delicate and colorful wings that Kokopelli had ever beheld, and he could see that it was dying.

The butterfly's wings were like spun silk, shimmering with reds, blues, greens, violets, yellows, and every other color imaginable marked by speckles, stripes and designs that Kokopelli had never seen before. The butterfly didn't move, except for a slight frightened shiver of its wings. As he moved his face closer to get a better look at the lovely butterfly, he could see that the edges of its wings were tattered from flitting against the bars of the cage for so long. The butterfly was very scared, and to Kokopelli it was obvious that it was nearing death from struggling to escape for so long. The powerful forces of nature had drawn it toward the outside air, like the power of a full moon pulling on the oceans, blue and deep. But the struggle against the cage bars had finally exhausted the butterfly, and it no longer had the strength to try to escape. Kokopelli's eyes filled with tears as he helplessly looked at the frightened butterfly. One of his eyes overflowed, and a large tear fell down his face and onto one of its wings. As it rolled down the butterfly's wing, nobody but Kokopelli saw what happened next. Amazingly, the butterfly's colors brightened in the wet trail left by the teardrop. And as it slowly flowed to the bottom of its wing, he saw the torn, uneven edge magically heal. His eyes widened with disbelief!

When the teardrop finally fell from the edge of the butterfly's wing, Kokopelli snapped out of the trance he was in and gazed at the many faces surrounding him. Every member of the tribe stared at him, smiling as if asking for his approval.

Kokopelli's trembling hands slowly lifted the cage as his eyes narrowed in grief. He ached with sadness because of the cruelty these people exhibited toward the butterfly. Through his tearful eyes, he looked at the people around him. The tribespeople saw this and the smiles on their faces quickly changed to expressions of confusion as they lowered their eyes from Kokopelli's gaze.

"Shame on you, Chief" Kokopelli said, his voice barely a whisper. "This creature is no different than you or me. It needs to be free and loved! Can't you see you've almost killed it? Please, let me release this butterfly back to nature where it belongs, right now!" he begged.

His request deeply angered the chief. "How dare you speak of letting my treasure go!" he screamed. He then ordered his men to seize Kokopelli and the butterfly!

At this moment Kokopelli knew what must be done. He was a peaceful man and therefore refused to fight. Kokopelli also knew that he and the butterfly might be harmed if they stayed, noticing a spear in the hands of one of the chief's men. Being a magician, he conjured a spell, creating a huge plume of thick, white smoke between the tribespeople and himself. He did this only to distract the tribe as he quickly and carefully clutched the cage to his chest and disappeared in the confusion. He just couldn't bring himself to leave the helpless butterfly behind to die. He hoped that one day he could help the tribe understand his actions, and called this out over his shoulder as he ran.

Kokopelli ran faster than he had ever run in his entire life, gently cradling the cage and the butterfly within. He ran so fast, the forest trees began to blur in his vision. He ran like this for miles and miles, taking care not to upset the cage and its precious contents.

Hours later, when he was far away from the village and was sure that no one would be able to find them, Kokopelli slowed and finally stopped next to a babbling stream and placed the cage on a cool, flat rock.

He moved cautiously so as not to scare the gentle butterfly, and slowly opened the cage. The butterfly did not appear frightened, but actually looked healthier and even more colorful as it slowly began to creep toward the door. Just then a surprising thing began to happen.

A female deer and her fawn approached the clearing, and the excited chatter of the forest's birds quieted as the butterfly began to move. A few rabbits stopped their evening meal so they could get a glimpse, with a mother fox and her pups standing next to them! A wolf stepped aside to let a squirrel family see, as a moose stood proudly over a badger. He noticed a grizzly bear shading a mother duck and her babies, as a lynx squeezed in next to a boar to watch this occasion. Even the fish jumped from the surface of the stream to look, while eagles perched above them for a better view. None of the animals minded when even the skunk and porcupine moved into the clearing! There were wild horses, snakes, bats, frogs, geese, and dozens of other animals sitting peacefully together. Kokopelli intuitively knew that the animals must hold a special place in their hearts for this butterfly.

Kokopelli lowered his hand to the opened cage door, and the butterfly slowly stepped onto his finger. Its brilliant wings began to open and close repeatedly as it gained confidence.

"Don't be afraid, beautiful butterfly, nobody will hurt you anymore" Kokopelli said softly.

The butterfly's wings began to open and close more quickly, and as it crouched, Kokopelli smiled. He knew the butterfly wanted to fly.

"Are you ready?" he asked.

With that, he stretched his hand skyward, and the butterfly flapped its large wings with great force. As its wings pulled through the air, the butterfly released his hand and began to fly upward. Kokopelli and the animals watched as the butterfly flew higher and higher toward the setting sun. As it flew, its wings shed a shimmering rainbow of scales as they instantly healed. The butterfly was even more lovely than before as its fresh colors reflected the orange light of the sunset, the beautiful rainbow created by its healing wings trailing behind it. Kokopelli and his animal friends watched quietly for quite some time as it flew far away toward the distant horizon.

Kokopelli shed a tear of happiness, relieved that the precious butterfly was finally free. He was also a bit sad because it was now so far away. He felt a magical bond had grown between them, and now the butterfly was gone. However, the butterfly was back in nature, healed and flying freely, and that was what mattered most. Kokopelli could tell by looking at the animals that they were grateful to him.

As if a spell was broken, the animals slowly returned to the forest, leaving Kokopelli alone with his thoughts.

He sat on the rock awhile, reflected on his amazing day, and watched the last of the breathtaking sunset alone. He was exhausted from the day's events, so he decided to make camp right where he was. It was a warm night, and all he needed for a bed were the soft leaves of the forest floor. The soothing song of the crickets and the babbling of the nearby stream relaxed him with their lullaby. Beneath a giant tree, he soon drifted into a sound sleep, comfortably nestled in the protective arms of Mother Earth.

Early the next morning he was awakened by the excited calls of the forest animals. As he rubbed the sleep from his eyes, he looked up and saw that his animal friends were again gathering in the clearing.

As he stood and brushed the leaves off himself, he saw that the animals were all looking in the same direction, *away* from Kokopelli. As he saw the object of their gaze, he couldn't believe his eyes. He was filled with wonderment at what stood before him. For standing in front of Kokopelli was a woman... but not just *any* woman. She was the most lovely woman Kokopelli had ever seen. He stood frozen with shy admiration, but her loving eyes and warm smile immediately soothed him. As they gazed at each other, he noticed something familiar about the way the forest animals had gathered.

Smiling, he asked "Who are you, fair lady?"

"Come closer, Kokopelli, and find out for yourself," she said softly with a shy grin. Kokopelli's heart was pounding. How did she know his name?

"Don't you recognize me?" she playfully asked.

"Should I?" he replied, searching his memory. He couldn't believe that he didn't remember a woman as interesting as she, yet there *was* something curiously familiar about her.

"Please come closer and take my hand," she said. He politely took her hand into his own and gently kissed it. He closed his eyes as he did this. When he opened them he was gazing directly into her eyes, and he smiled knowingly.

The irises of her eyes glowed red, blue, green, violet, yellow, and all the colors in between, shining with unmatched radiance in the morning sun.

Amazed, Kokopelli asked, "You're the butterfly, aren't you?"

She smiled at this and nodded her head, her breathtaking eyes brilliant in the sun's warm glow.

"You broke a terrible spell when you released me from that cage, Kokopelli," she explained. "When I was a very little girl I wandered away from my family and became lost. I spent a terribly frightening night in the woods alone...

ut I was found and raised peacefully over the years by the forest's animals. They took turns nurturing and protecting me, teaching me to love and respect all living things."

"Many years later, the chief of the tribe you ran from ordered me captured when he saw me playfully wrestling with my wolf brothers and sisters. He became frightened, because his ancestors believed only evil spirits could survive playing with wild animals. When they looked closely at me, they became even more afraid, because the rainbow color of my eyes was not like theirs. They feared me because I looked and behaved differently."

"**S**o the medicine man cast a spell and transformed me into a butterfly. By changing me into the most delicate of the animals, they then felt I could do them no harm. I wish I could have explained that I was part of the animals' family and would *never* harm any living thing, but I was not allowed the chance. I had been in that cage for over twenty years when you found me. Thank you, Kokopelli," she said, with love in her voice and eyes.

Kokopelli knew that for the first time, he was in love. Although he didn't even know her name, he felt that she could be the woman he had been thinking of for so long. He told her this, as a powerful feeling of love filled his pounding heart. She felt the same way, and told him so.

As he stared lovingly into her eyes he asked, "What is your name, beautiful butterfly?"

"My name is Samsara," she replied. Her animal family loudly voiced their pleasure at the sound of her name, as they had missed her so very much.

"Samsara," Kokopelli said to himself, as a nice, warm feeling washed over him. He felt as if he had known this woman forever, and hoped that he would. He had finally found the woman of his dreams. Destiny had brought them together and her expression reflected his emotions.

"Where shall we go?" she asked, eager to explore.

"When the time is right, and only if you wish it so, could we go back one day and make peace with that tribe? We could bring them a gift to show that you are *not* an evil spirit, but a caring woman who is friends with the animals," he replied.

"Yes, Kokopelli, I would like that very much. But where shall we go right *now*?" she asked, smiling playfully.

"Well, around the world and back again, if that's all right with you," he said. She agreed happily as she looked lovingly into his eyes. Kokopelli's heart leapt with joy when she looked at him, and he fell more deeply in love with this gentle woman every moment.

They laughed and held hands as they walked into the forest. True to their word, Kokopelli and Samsara *did* go back and make peace with that tribe, and all was forgiven. They *did* travel all over the world, growing their love for each other and spreading loving kindness to all the people they met.

Kokopelli had finally found his princess, and he knew that they would live happily ever after.

Thank you for supporting a self-published author!

To order additional copies of <u>Kokopelli & the Butterfly</u>

Send a check or money order for $19.95 (Florida residents add 7% sales tax)
+ $3.00 shipping and handling to:

Grasshopper Dream Productions
P.O. Box 1831
St. Petersburg, FL 33731-1831

or, please neatly print your Visa or Mastercard number, expiration date
and name as it appears on the card and send to the above address.

or, go to **www.kokopelli-butterfly.com**

Don't forget to mention how you would like the author to autograph your book!